PENGUINAUT!

WRITTEN BY **Marcie Colleen**   ILLUSTRATED BY **Emma Yarlett**

To Mom and Dad, for being my launch pad. —Marcie

For Isaiah and Solomon, —love Emma

First published in 2018 by Orchard Books
An imprint of Scholastic Inc.

This edition published in the UK in 2018
by Scholastic Children's Books
Euston House, 24 Eversholt Street
London NW1 1DB, UK
A division of Scholastic Ltd
www.scholastic.co.uk
London ~ New York ~ Toronto ~ Sydney ~ Auckland
Mexico City ~ New Delhi ~ Hong Kong

Text copyright © Marcie Colleen 2018
Illustrations copyright © Emma Yarlett, 2018

ISBN 978 1407 19657 2

The text type was set in Warnock Pro Bold.
The title type was hand-lettered by Emma Yarlett.
The illustrations were done in watercolor, collage,
pencil, crayon, pen, and paint.

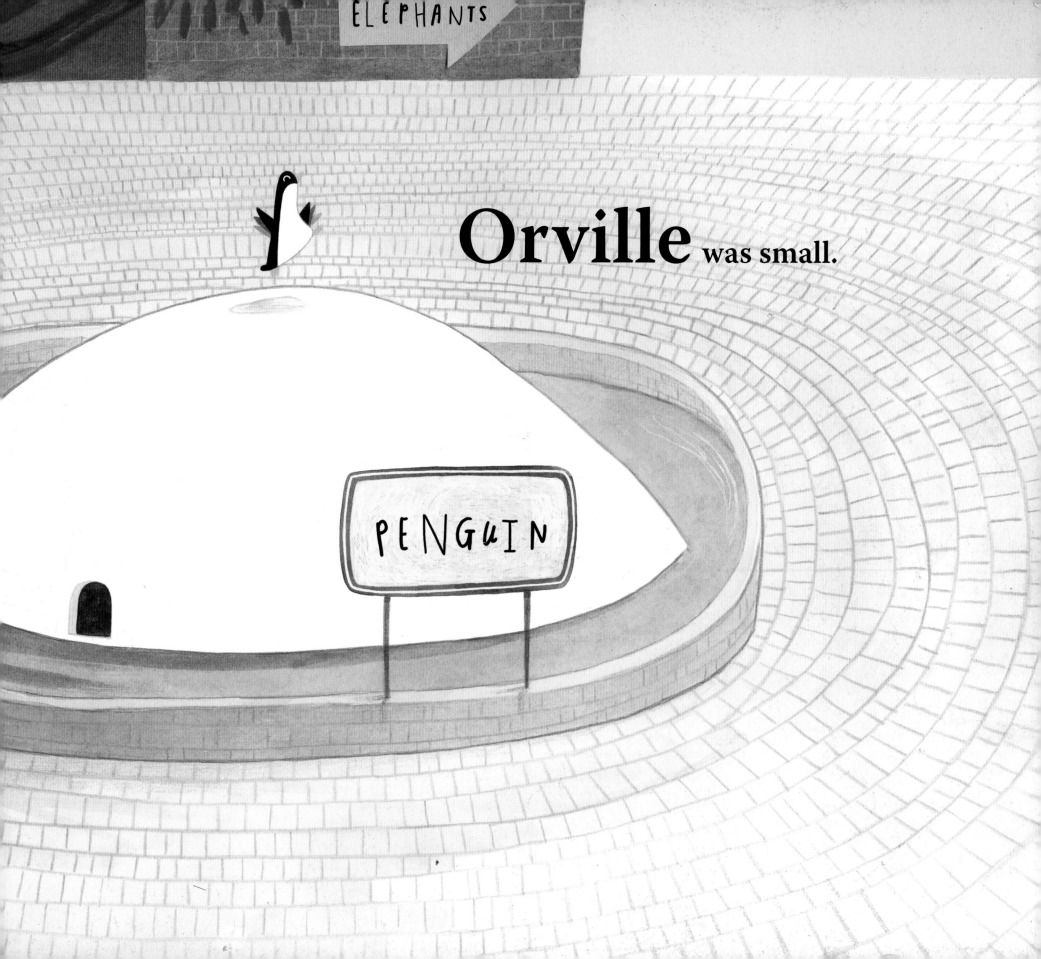

ELEPHANTS

Orville was small.

PENGUIN

His friends were BIG.

And their

adventures

were **BIGGER.**

Orville longed for *big* adventures, too.

One day, he announced his plans for the **biggest** and best adventure yet.

Orville flippered out.

He tried to flap — KERPLOP!

He tried to climb — WHACK!

He tried to catapult — fa-LING!

. . . and landed in the reptile house.
Orville was pretty sure the
boa constrictor was not trying to hug him.

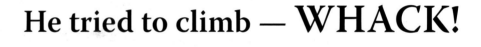

Still Orville kept trying.

He borrowed from
the zookeeper.
He nicked from
the trash cans.
He built and built.

And with

a **shake,**

shake,

shake

of a half-filled

soda bottle,

the ship

was

ready

for

liftoff.

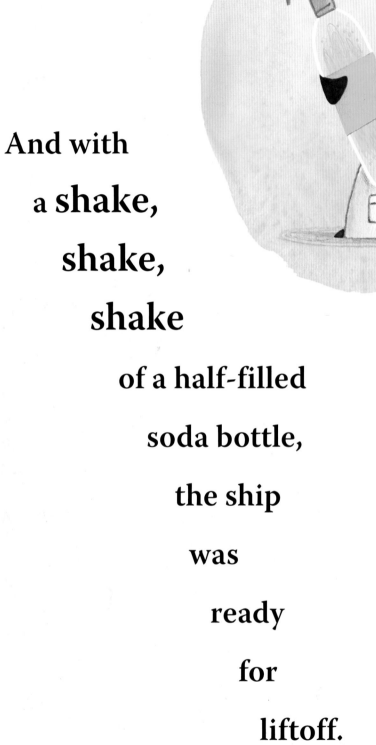

It was perfect.

And perfectly

penguin-sized.

With a trembling flipper salute,

he took his place at the controls.

WHOOSH!

The ship zipped through the night sky,

through clouds, over stars,

and straight to the moon.

Orville landed.

His stomach
felt queasy.
His spacesuit
felt squeezy.
Now that
he'd made it,
what would
he do?

He took a small step.

He hopped.

Did a little dance.

And tripped.

TUMBLE BUMBLE

He somersaulted with stars,

cartwheeled over craters,

BA BOING!

and giggled for all the galaxy to hear.

It was the BIGGEST and best adventure yet.

"I'm doing it myself!" he cheered,

but his tiny voice was swallowed up

in the starry blackness.

Orville stopped.

He was all alone.

His stomach grew queasier.

His spacesuit grew squeezier.

He shivered

and a note fell out

of his pocket.

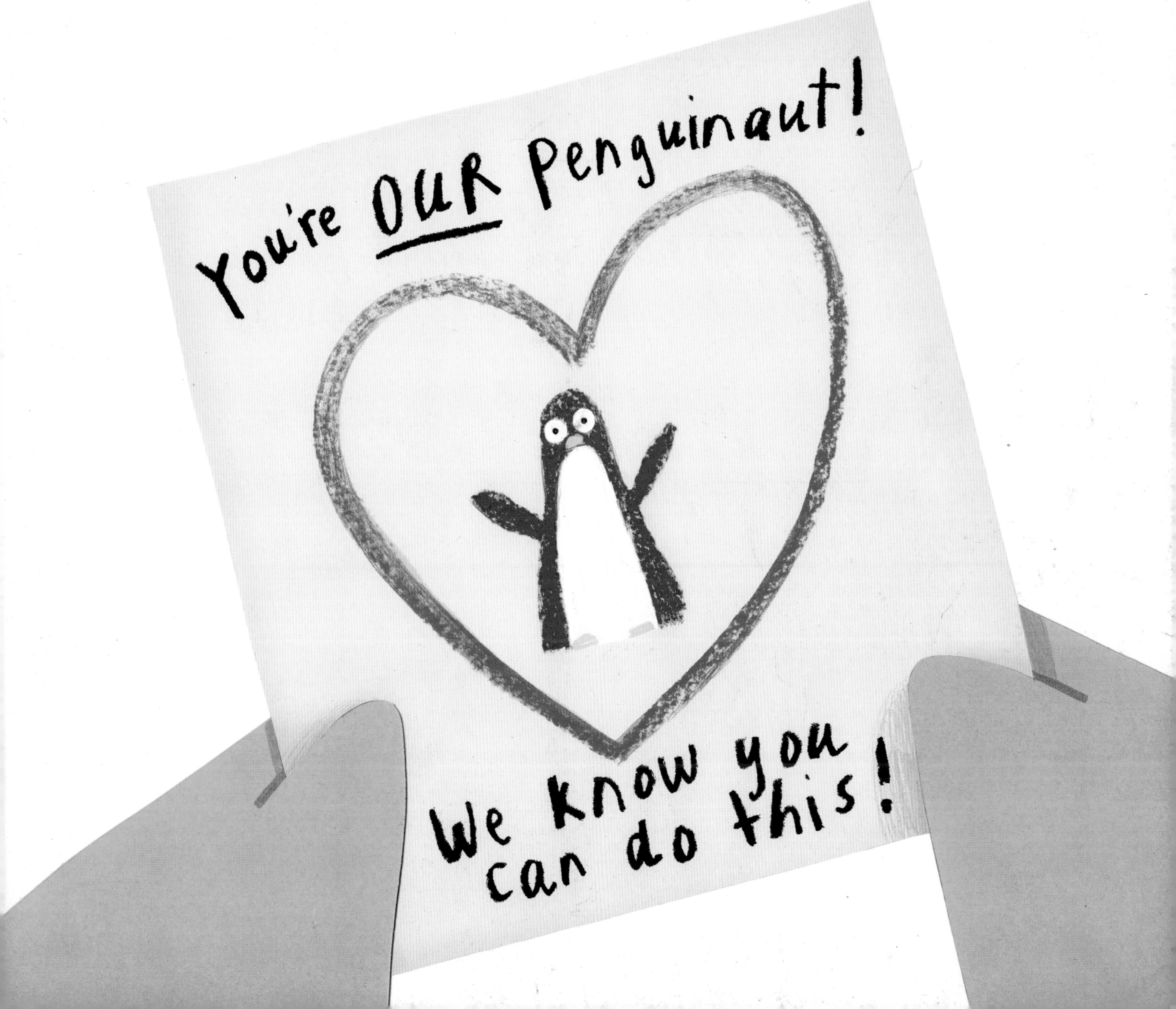
You're OUR Penguinaut!
We know you can do this!

He missed his friends.

So Orville
closed his eyes
tightly
and imagined
they were
there.

When he was safely back in his ship,

he looked toward home.

He couldn't wait to tell everyone

about his **big** adventure.

Sure, Orville's friends
were BIG.
Now the proud Penguinaut
felt BIG, too.

But BIGGEST of all?

Being together
was out
of this world.

3, 2, 1 . . .

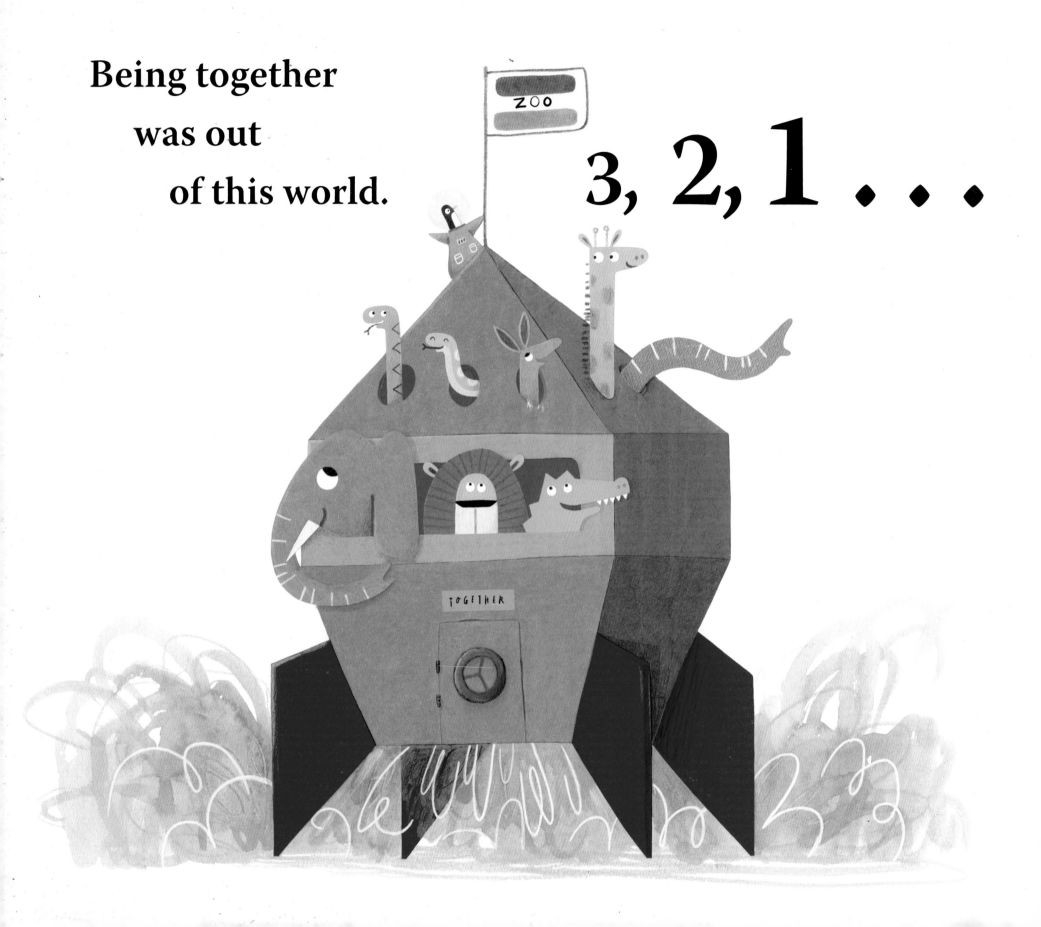